FANTASTIC
ORGY

FANTASTIC

TRANSLATED BY

W. C. BAMBERGER

ALEXANDER M.

FREY

WAKEFIELD PRESS

ORGY

CAMBRIDGE, MASSACHUSETTS

Wakefield Press, P.O. Box 425645, Cambridge, MA 02142

Originally published in German as *Phantastische Orgie* in 1924.

This book was set in Garamond Premier Pro and Helvetica Neue Pro by Wakefield Press. Printed and bound by Versa Press in the United States of America.

ISBN: 978-1-939663-94-8

Available through D.A.P./Distributed Art Publishers
75 Broad Street, Suite 630
New York, New York 10004
Tel: (212) 627-1999
Fax: (212) 627-9484

10   9   8   7   6   5   4   3   2   1

CONTENTS

TRANSLATOR'S INTRODUCTION

Alexander Moritz Frey was born 29 March 1881 in Munich. His father, Wilhelm Frey (1826–1911), was nearly fifty when Alexander was born. Wilhelm, originally from Switzerland, was a sometime opera singer and a painter. He married Alexander's mother, Sophie Block (1842–1918), a year after his first wife died. Sophie was from a military family. Frey later described his mother as constantly ailing, religious to the point of bigotry, socially conservative, and domineering.[1]

Alexander was the couple's only child. He attended a Protestant elementary school in Munich, and later the Luitpold Gymnasium. He disliked his school years: "Overburdened with learning, we students were simply pack mules, driven on by the beatings of teachers."[2] In 1895, the family moved to Mannheim, where Wilhelm became the director of the Grand Ducal picture gallery. The family lived in servants' quarters in Mannheim Castle. "We lived in sky-high, armchair-sized rooms," Frey later wrote to Thomas Mann.[3] Frey graduated in 1903 and hoped to study medicine at university.

His parents, however, compelled him to study law. After three and a half years at the Universities of Heidelberg, Freiburg, and Munich, he failed the state legal exam in a spectacular fashion: He turned in blank sheets of paper.

Frey took up residence in Munich and became a journalist and writer. In 1909 he read from the manuscript of his novel-in-progress *Soleneman der Unsichtbare* (Solenman the unseen) to a small audience that included Thomas Mann.[4] From this encounter, Frey and Mann developed a friendship that lasted the rest of Mann's life. When the Nazis came into power and Frey had to go into exile, Mann helped support him financially. In 1955, the year he died, Mann wrote a foreword to Frey's book *Kleine Menagerie* (Little menagerie). In it he speaks of Frey as a man "of profound steadfastness, understanding, calm, and goodness, with whom I have been on good terms for decades."[5] Frey was also friends with Heinrich Mann, theater director Max Reinhart, and the artists Franz Marc and Hans Arp.

While still at school, Frey had begun writing and submitting his work. He published his first poem, "Musik," in 1907, in *Wertermanns Monats-Heften*; other poems appeared in anthologies such as *Neue Deutsche Poems* (1908) and *Stimmungen* (1909). His first stories began appearing in 1910.

In 1913, Frey's first book was published: *Dunkle Gänge: Zwölf Geschichten aus Nacht und Schatten* (Dark passages: Twelve stories of night and shadow).[6] These stories—fantastic and mystical, surreal and macabre grotesques that resemble dreams or expeditions into the unconscious—employ many of the conventions of horror stories; but at the same time, as a 1984 dissertation by Katrin Hoffmann-Walbeck observes, a significant portion of his work exhibits "a more harmless playful character in which the enjoyment of comic intricacy and punch lines predominates."[7]

Solneman der Unsichtbare, which has become Frey's best-known novel, was published in 1914. A mysterious stranger, Hciebel Solneman (German for "I live nameless," reversed), who always hides his face behind a mask, approaches the administration of a small city and buys the city park for an enormous sum. He then encloses it within an enormously high wall. He wants to be "alone, interred—unseen." He trucks in furniture and exotic animals, but no townspeople are allowed to see inside the walls. Hans J. Schütz describes what ensues:

> Solneman, a phantom who evades the curiosity of the citizens, throws the entire city into turmoil and outrage. His mysterious existence provokes the citizens of the small town to the point where they give him no rest. . . . The conflict between the oddball, the dreamer and utopian and the bourgeoisie, between the individual and the state, is Frey's subject, and not just in *Solneman*. The symbol of this antagonism is the wall around Solneman's Estate, which he leaves to the city as an indelible relic after he disappears.[8]

In addition to several volumes of stories, Frey followed *Solneman* with the tragic novel *Kastan und die Dirnen* in 1918. *Robinsonade zu Zwoelft* (1925), a bitingly satirical and grotesque novel set partly in China, again took up the Solneman theme.

Many German writers were enthusiastic about the First World War, but Frey did not share in this widespread patriotic enthusiasm. He remained a pacifist but joined the army. From 1915 to 1918 he served as a medic in the trenches on the Western Front together with the dispatcher Adolf Hitler. Later, Frey's former "comrade-in-arms" repeatedly encouraged him to join the National Socialists, a request that Frey firmly rejected.[9] In 1929, Frey published *Die Pflasterkästen*, an autobiographical antiwar novel based on his experiences tending to victims of the war during his three-year deployment. The novel is much more realistic and sober in style than Frey's earlier works. Some contemporary critics considered it superior to Remarque's *Im Westen nichts Neues* (*All Quiet on the Western Front*). The book was highly praised by such critics as Salomo Friedlaender and W. E. Süskind, but its publication also led to polemics against the author. The book was later included in the list of books the Nazis did not approve of and was among those they burned.

Die Pflasterkästen appeared in English in 1931 as *The Cross Bearers*.[10] A reviewer for *Newsweek* considered it a standout in a market filled "to the saturation point" with war books:

> Though far from being a record of unrelieved horrors, it shows war's seamiest side, and with open seams. . . . Even less politely written than *All Quiet on the Western Front*, *The Cross Bearers* mentions words, things not usually mentioned, [and] in its own way does its bit to illuminate war.[11]

Frey's only other book previously published in English was of a very different sort. This was *The Stout-Hearted Cat: A Fable for Cat Lovers* (1947). Here Birl the cat's adventures include being tattooed and feathered and being forced to become part of a circus freak show before she escapes and is happily reunited with her owner.

On 15 March 1933, a few hours before his house was to be raided by the Nazi Party's paramilitary wing the SA, Frey was warned of their coming and was able to escape to Austria in the trunk of a friend's car. He spent five years in Salzburg and the last twenty years of his life in Basel. When Frey arrived in Switzerland in 1938 he was almost sixty years old, and as he could not claim to have been persecuted on racial or political grounds, the Swiss, wary of provoking their militaristic neighbor, refused to grant him any legal status within the country. He lived in difficult conditions, barely making enough to live on as he conducted a long legal feud with the Swiss authorities. He was subjected to harassment by the police and by army censors. He managed to scrape by, doing his best to keep his work low-profile enough not to attract the notice of the Swiss authorities, who had forbidden him to work in the country. He was nevertheless repeatedly threatened with expulsion.

Frey published a few more books after 1945, some of which critics felt showed that his narrative powers had waned. He wrote two long novels: the antiwar novel *Der Gefallene steht auf* (The fallen one stands up), which remains unpublished, and *Hölle und Himmel* (Hell and heaven), which was published in Zurich in 1945. In *Hölle und Himmel*, "Frey dealt with Hitler in a fictional manner and analyzed the motives of the Nazis with the means of the fantastic."[12]

At the time of his death, Frey had been working on a sequel to *Solneman*.

In 1954, Frey's naturalization application was officially rejected because he was "not sufficiently assimilated."[13] He died in

Basel on 24 January 1957, a few days after the city had finally granted him citizenship. An obituary in the *Süddeutsche Zeitung* (28 January) offered this portrait:

> Not many will remember, for it was thirty years ago that a small, dainty gentleman first plied his trade in Munich writers' circles. . . . He usually sat on the sidelines and didn't say much, but he let his strikingly clear, large eyes roam all the more attentively in his cool, clever ram's face. The scrupulously correctly dressed figure, the iron back, the sandy-blond hair pointed to a surgeon or a lawyer, certainly not to the author of fantastic, bizarre stories full of mystifications.[14]

* * *

The title story here first appeared in 1920—as "Orgie"—in *Der Neue Merkur*.[15] It was retitled "Phantastische Orgie" ("Fantastic Orgy") when it was reprinted in an eponymous collection in 1924.[16] The three other stories translated here were also included in this edition, though "Opfer" ("Offering") had also been included in Frey's previous collection, *Der Unheimliche Abend* (The eerie night), the year before.

"Fantastic Orgy" presents not a titillating commingling of human bodies but the troubled postwar commingling of human body and technology, endemic to the Weimar era in the maimed veterans of World War I and the unsettled fantasies of female automatons, controlled and otherwise. The image of a will-less human being under the control of an abusive master was very much in the air in Weimar Germany. The year "Orgie" first appeared was also the year the films *The Cabinet of Caligari* and *The Golem* were released. Fritz Lang's *Metropolis*, with its nightmarish confusion of woman and robot, and violent confrontation between exploited labor and greedy owners, appeared in 1927. Some critics speculate this was an effect of the dehumanizing treatment of both soldiers and civilians in the war years, and the hardships endured during the rebuilding period that followed, as well. The part-woman-part-machine figure was also present in the art and literature of the period.[17] John Heartfield and Hannah Höch were just two of the many artists who created assemblages and photo collages with such images. "Fantastic Orgy" weaves together all these elements: the female-or-machine figure under the control of an exploiter, bonding with men damaged and impoverished by the war.

The compassion for the exploited and the poor that Frey evidences in "Fantastic Orgy" is also present in the other three stories here. But the combination of dry humor, compassion, sharp-eyed cultural and psychological observation, the macabre, and great powers of invention found in this collection is also present in varying proportions in Frey's other stories and novels. It is to be hoped that the publication of *Fantastic Orgy* will encourage more translations of his work.

NOTES

1. Katrin Hoffman-Walbeck, "Alexander Moritz Frey—(Allegorisch) Phantastik und Groteske als Mittel der Zeitkritik," dissertation (Frankfurt am Main, 1984), quoted in Ernsting. A list of frequently cited secondary sources can be found at the end of this introduction. All translations from sources are my own.

2. Frey's CV, ca. 1939. Quoted in Ernsting.

3. Hoffman-Walbeck, 78. Quoted in Ernsting.

4. "Solneman" is *namenlos* (German for "nameless") spelled backward.

5. Quoted in in Schütz, 68.

6. *Dunkle Gänge: Zwölf Geschichten aus Nacht und Schatten* (Munich: Delphin). I have seen the date of this first publication given as 1912 but it appears that 1913 is correct.

7. Hoffman-Walbeck, 77. Quoted in Ernsting, part one.

8. Schütz, 67.

9. After Frey's death, a manuscript was discovered wherein Frey details his experiences serving with Hitler. He describes how Hitler's moustache took on its distinctive shape when he was ordered to trim it to better ensure the fit of his gas mask.

10. *The Cross Bearers* (London: Putnam, 1931); no translator credited.

11. Anon., "Books: Little Reminder," *Newsweek*, 20 October 1930. https://content.time.com/time/subscriber/article/0,33009,740620,00.html.

12. Ernsting, part one.

13. Schütz, 70.

14. Quoted in Ernsting.

15. *Der Neue Merkur* 4, Berlin 1920.

16. *Phantastische Orgie* (Ludwigsburg: Chronos Verlag, 1924).

17. An interesting study of this movement is Matthew Biro, *The Dada Cyborg: Vision of the New Human in Weimar Berlin* (Minneapolis: University of Minnesota Press, 2009).

SELECTED BIBLIOGRAPHY OF FREY'S PUBLISHED BOOKS

Dunkle Gänge: Zwölf Geschichten aus Nacht und Schatten. Munich: Delphin Verlag, 1913.

Solneman der Unsichtbare. Munich: Delphin Verlag, 1914.

Sprünge: Dreizehn Grotesken. Stuttgart: Wagner Verlag, 1922.

Der Unheimliche Abend. Munich: Kurt Wolff Verlag, 1923.

Phantastische Orgie. Ludwigsburg: Chronos Verlag, 1924.

Außenseiter: Zwölf seltsame Geschichten. Munich: Drei Masken Verlag, 1927.

Die Pflasterkästen: Ein Feldsanitätsroman. Berlin: Gustav Kiepenheuer, 1929.

The Cross Bearers. London: Putnam, 1931. No translator credited.

The Stout-Hearted Cat: A Fable for Cat Lovers. Translated by Richard and Clara Winston. New York: Henry Holt, 1947. (Also published as *Birl: The Story of a Cat*. London: Jonathan Cape, 1948.)

SOURCES

Ernsting, Stefan. "Der phantastische Rebell Alexander Moritz Frey, oder Hitler schießt dramatisch in die Luft." *Perlentaucher*, 29 January 2007. https://shorturl.at/SZhMf (accessed 2 January 2023).

Frenschkowski, Marco. "Spuk des Alltags: Ein Nachwort." In Alexander Moritz Frey, *Spuk des Alltags* (Neubrandenburg: Blitz Verlag, 2004), 231–239.

Schütz, Hans J. "Frey, Alexander Moritz." In Hans J. Schütz, *Ein Deutscher Dichter bin ich einst gewesen* (Munich: C. H. Beck Verlag, 1988), 66–71.

Seefried, Romina. "Phantoma, Mensch oder Maschine?—Zur Entgrenzung und Technisierung des künstlichen Körpers in der Literatur der Frühen Moderne." In *Überwindung der Körperlichkeit. Historische Perspektiven auf den künstlichen Körper*, ed. Dominik Groß and Ylva Söderfeldt (Kassel: Kassel University Press), 15–34.

Seefried, Romina. "'Welch schamlose Bestie der Krieg ist': Zu Leben und Werk des Schriftstellers Alexander Moritz Frey." *REAL: Revista de Estudos Alemães*, no. 5, August 2014. https://shorturl.at/be1jj (accessed 2 January 2023).

Wolff, Joachim Manfred. "Nachwort." In A. M. Frey, *Solneman der Unsichtbare* (Frankfurt am Main: Suhrkamp Verlag, 1990), 223–229.

FANTASTIC
ORGY

———

The beggar sat on the ground, leaning against a lamppost that dogs had been pissing on for a generation.

Konrad wanted to pass by him as he passed all things: hesitantly and with a stifled longing in his blood to stop and surrender.

The beggar noticed this and turned his dust-veiled gaze upward. The first link in the chain of organists who had lined up along the Street Fair curb, he was about to change the record in his music box. He let it go with a clatter and snapped his hat up to just below Konrad's navel.

Konrad, who had already hurled himself half past, staggered, tripped up by the gesture, saved himself by turning—and helplessly fingered his pockets and wallet.

The beggar saw his victory, let the superfluous hat clap back on the street, and applied himself again to the organ to torture it further. When he saw a two-mark note fluttering down between his fumbling hands, he fell into an assured line of patter: If the gentleman would wait a moment, he would hear Liszt's "Liebeslust." From three to six o'clock it was always "Ich Weiss Nicht, was Soll es Bedeuten"; but now, from six until eight, it was "Liebeslust."

Konrad pretended to be ready to indulge in "Liebeslust." With one unsteady hand, the beggar clamped the disc in position. Konrad reddened without moving to help when he saw how the man came to the rescue of his remaining three fingers by pressing down with his forehead and nose. Then the crank, in the odd grip of his claws, whizzed around. The beggar carefully listened to his own performance, and Konrad was able to steal away.

So many barrel organs, all reinforcing one another! The expelled breath of one taken in by the next and passed on to the third.

So many kinds of cripples, each spinning music from a whirling wooden box, so that it flew up, whipped by anxiety, to race its way, high and wild, over the tent booths with their chimes and speakers. Konrad passed along this string of beggars aligned in the gutter who kept a precisely maintained equal distance between them, as if clinging to the last of the martial discipline and former greatness of the fatherland—walked past them as if he were in some way getting the better of them—and gained the square with the booths.

A storm cloud, rushing down darkly, hastily tore through the autumn evening down onto the tents. The booths swayed wildly, small and dancing in gusts of wind, ships whose canvas crackled and snapped. Poles broke and struck rigging with a thud. Banknotes fluttered from a cash register and shot, pale gulls, into the squall.

With shouts from the people below, colored lights, blood-red or yellow in the twilight, soared high, and immediately swung in time to the dance of the storm.

Konrad escaped the first raindrops, which fell heavily at threatening intervals, by climbing up into one of the billowing booths. He boarded the ship over a swaying stairway. As he entrusted a mark to the till that had been robbed by the storm, he saw that it had been christened "Phantomata." He pushed through a curtain that was futilely scurrying in the wind and entered its belly.

It was already filled with refugees who hoped for little from this small stage but everything from the canvas cover, bowed by hammering water, over their heads.

"Phantomata, human or machine?"

The impresario, overwhelmed by the influx that broke in like a torrent as a result of the pounding rain, and despite the updraft of banknotes, over which he cursed the cashier through a curtain, was immediately ready to show his wonder.

"Phantomata, gentlemen, human or machine, female riddle for all scholars of civilized lands. A highly honored audience will see for themselves that they do not know what she is. What might she be—the greatest miracle of hypnosis, or the mechanical masterpiece of all time? I will now start the experiments, and I ask for your complete attention. I will have the honor of presenting Phantomata in three acts. In the first act you will see the most curious manifestations of life by the human machine in response to my commands. I will now begin."

The man, in his red tailcoat, knee breeches, and riding boots, tore aside a greasy background curtain and, wheezing, lifted a glass-eyed woman from a little cupboard-like cabinet by wrapping his arms around her rigid limbs. Dragging her out in this manner, he raised her toward the curious crowd. Phantomata rested tensely, leaning a bit forward, trembling a little due to her mechanism, like an object teetering on an edge. Konrad quietly doubted that this was any sort of human being.

After an enigmatic invocation and some manipulation, Phantomata made her way across the three-pace-wide stage with staring eyes and stiff feet. A length of wire that emerged from her spine and ended at an ankle cuff trailed behind her.

What . . . ? Does the machine energize itself from the waist into the leg? Konrad wavered—then the man in the red tailcoat lifted and turned his lifeless machine, which was shuffling with her nose against the wall, and let her traverse the tiny stage again in mechanical, trembling steps. Let her raise and lower her arms with the white woolen gloves semaphorically, bend at the waist and straighten up, and project her painted plaster head into every gloomy corner of the tent. Golden curls danced, innocent and moving, like some lost living thing, over a forehead behind which nothing lived.

Behind which nothing lived? Konrad asked himself uneasily. He looked closely at the air vents of the machine: no warm haze emerged from the nostrils in the damp, cold autumn evening.

The impresario in his riding boots crossed over to Phantomata in her white dancing shoes and dragged her all the way to the ramp. Phantomata then stood there as the man in the red tailcoat manipulated her, positioning her arms as he wished. He dug a bottle out of his coat, unscrewed the screeching plug, and passed its vapor under Phantomata's nostrils.

Konrad saw how the girl's gaze seemed to return from a distant stare, to come back to the booth. Two eyelids with thick lashes went down like curtains, behind which the empty stage was now supposed to come to life. When they shot back up again, Konrad saw himself and everyone else there performing in the background of the eyes above them, eyes that pulsed greetings down into the audience.

"This was the first section, ladies and gentlemen! Before I sink Fräulein Phantomata into deep sleep again, so that she can undertake some new dance creations in the second section, and also so that you can convince yourself that Phantomata is a person made of flesh and blood, she will now come down to you in the auditorium. She will sell you her picture postcard as a souvenir and ask for a small additional payment. It should be noted that Phantomata expends an extraordinary amount of mental and psychological energy in these performances, which are repeated twenty times a day. The heavy toll taken on her nervous system means that in five years' time she will be completely incapable of working and will likely remain so forever. For this reason, and for the difficult time that lies ahead for her, Phantomata asks you to support her as best you can."

She came down a chicken ladder and slipped through row after row, the postcards fanned out in her hands. At times she got stuck due to the wire that floated behind her and which, awestricken, no one dared to touch.

But she stopped, startled, because a hunchback's voice rose from the standing-room area, where Konrad also stood. The hunchback pointed to her and, more violently, to the drowsy-looking idle man in the red coat above them, and then began shouting: "Will we tolerate the fact that over the next five years this girl will slowly be ruined?! If anything cries out to heaven it is this greedy gentleman's scheme involving this defenseless one. Will no one rebel against a disgrace that is being done to all people through this girl? We should help, we should join forces to free this half-lost woman from the clutches of this bloodsucker."

Some laughed at the temper and sharp demeanor of the hotheaded hunchback, others remained undecided;

many grumbled and demanded the resumption of the spectacle for which they had paid their one mark. Under the renewed hammering of water, they twisted and groaned incessantly. In the drum roll of the cloudburst, pressed together by it as closely as it was possible to be, uproar, placation, counterattack, and curiosity were all combined.

The impresario addressed him: "The gentleman there in the back meddles in things that are none of his business. You have paid a mark to see Phantomata perform. Fräulein Phantomata performs voluntarily and with all her mental faculties intact. If the gentleman wishes to further disrupt the performance, he will be removed in the interest of the other venerable attendees who have also paid. You, sir, can have the mark you paid returned at the cash register at any time! You are free to go! Go where you please, sir; just remove yourself from my establishment!"

Phantomata stood and smiled with lacquered cheeks. Her smile was forlorn, as if she had already been through those five years and was now finished, yet soothing, as if she were also striving to use herself and her art to retie all the broken threads of understanding. Her eyes moved from the man in the red tailcoat, over the rain-splattered crowd, to the hunchback, and back again.

The small, crooked man would not relent. He raised his immense ape-like arms toward the damp gray canopy of the booth and wailed as if in despair: "Why isn't everyone here shaking with sadness and rage?! Is murder prosecuted in this country or is it not? What is murder with a knife in five seconds compared to this murder, brutally dragged out over five years, with the result that the murdered one remains cruelly alive?" He knows, oh yes—he, whose hump is in his bruised throat and in every uncontrollably flailing joint, knows what it means to be physically ruined, and so spiritually without a comfortable dwelling. "The monstrous crimes against the bodies of millions over the last few years should not be allowed to be added to by this outrage, one which is so shocking because it is happening insidiously and for the sake of the basest greed."

Everyone was silent, surrounded by the soft drumming of the diminishing water. The desire to see the "dance creations" began to rise anew. Snorting, the man in the red tailcoat came down—the chicken ladder broke under his agitated weight—and grabbed the small man by the arm.

"You, sir, are leaving now! Here's your mark, your admission! You are leaving my establishment right this moment!"

But the hunchback resisted. He continued to fight, shrilly screaming that Phantomata should be spared from those five years of destruction. He went into a frenzy, with the sturdy forest of pant legs all around him. He was angrily seized by those who felt his hands indiscriminately pinching them, and, where a stretch of

FANTASTIC ORGY

the canvas on the shabby side wall had come loose in all the back and forth, he was unceremoniously bounced through the hole into the open, onto the meadow and into a rain puddle. The man in the red tailcoat concluded this interlude by hanging a piece of cloth over the gap.

There was grumbling laughter, but it soon subsided. A good-natured voice made a prediction: "Perhaps he has fallen on his hump and that will straighten out all his quirks."

Phantomata stood in front of Konrad and held out the cards to him. Her thick blonde hair was pushed up under her nightcap as if it were stuffed under a bowl; it sprang out of it and scrawled itself across her temples and neck, stuck to the tough greasy makeup on which it fell like a shimmering butterfly on flypaper. Konrad looked into her face: it had a faint reddish tint, as if the skin of an anemic had been artistically removed and the skinless face greased and polished. The front of her bonnet, the lace collar of her dressing gown, her white cotton gloves, showed intrusive traces of the greasy makeup under which Phantomata lived her life. He even saw it—inexplicably, and as if it were a devouring plague—on the toes of her dancing shoes.

Konrad bought some cards and asked: "Is it really that bad? What are you going to do after these five years have passed?" He looked into a face that wasn't one. It was perhaps only a millimeter deep under the makeup—but it was immeasurably far away. It was entirely expressionless. The eyes that were too big, too wet, were not in control of this wasteland.

A painted mouth spoke as if by rote: "Please, sir— one piece sixty pfennigs, two pieces one mark," and with an embarrassed smile refused to concede that it might not be that bad.

What is lying under this visibly shifting mask, under this thick casing made of pink pulp? Konrad asked himself. Does she get enough to eat? In how many ways—all in all—is this man in the red tailcoat abusing her? Do those riding boots sometimes kick her in the stomach? Can she take off her makeup at night or is she only allowed to sleep for short spells with her neck on a stool?— because make-up is expensive nowadays. What kind of creatures are they that turn barrel organs and cover their clothes with the dogs' urine of the lampposts? Who play "Liebeslust" every day from six to eight, but are unbudgeable from three to six o'clock? I don't know what all of this is supposed to mean.

Because the man in the red tailcoat up on the miniature stage began to promise what Phantomata would now perform in the second act, she was momentarily free of the circle of curious onlookers, and Konrad was able to deliver his invitation unmolested. He had to repeat it softly and with emphasis before she accepted. She agreed to it with an uncertain expression from which for a few seconds the stiffness emerged with which she was fitted out while working as Phantomata. It seemed to Konrad that she was easing the making of her decision through the small self-deception of having surrendered to his will and accepting his invitation as an order.

Konrad watched her avoid the trampled steps and land on the stage with a jump that bypassed the mass of men and stand ready. He saw the man in the tailcoat twisting the chirping stopper from the bottle, which had a sleeping or awakening effect as he chose; then he lifted up the remains of a curtain, closed it behind him, and as he passed the cashier, welcomed the immense autumn evening which breathed in on him through a small gap between the oilcloths. Konrad climbed down the gangway and swam out into the rain-swept night air.

The multiple lamps screamed at him no less furiously than did the rattle of the metal cymbals and kettledrums. After the storm had packed everyone together and brought things to a halt, they all now redoubled their howling at the clouds and into the dirt-free wind, which had maternally picked up all the new debris.

Konrad walked about, indecisive. He wanted to leave. He walked all around Phantomata's booth with a wire on his leg that held him tight. Do all the barrel organ men play "Liebeslust" from six to eight o'clock? I have to investigate.

He paced the line like an overseer. I'm just missing the lash, he thought, trying to grasp what was being cranked out. But the hats always got in the way, rising imploringly into the air and directing his attention to his own wallet.

The beggars all sat as they had been sitting before. A few appeared to have temporarily evaded the worst of the downpour. They had stretched their sweat-soaked jackets—more impenetrable than Konrad's raincoat—over the water-sensitive gears of their music machines, and they continued to crank on these hooded, now damped howling beasts. They themselves were dripping from the downpour. Their trouser legs splashed in the gutter; drops were gathered into little ponds in the pits of their oily faces.

What are they turning? What are they cranking? Why are they making such an incoherent muddle? Couldn't everyone, starting at the same speed, crank out "Liebeslust"? "Liebeslust" from six to eight o'clock, some thirty times in a row. How many are there? I count six along the street. I have already invited Phantomata; I must provide amusements for my unique guest.

And he asked the barrel organ player who had only three fingers to come that evening to number five Richtergasse, the ground floor, adding that he should bring his instrument and make music; there would also be something to eat and drink.

"I can't do it," he is told—unless he also brings along his neighbor there at the next lantern, the blind man.

They are dependent on one another and live together in the same barn.

Konrad considered this—somewhat like a commercial trader—and said that he can only bring the blind man with him. Would they both be able to play "Liebeslust" at the same time and would their boxes play at the same speed?

The beggar answered that the blind man does not have "Liebeslust"; but there, diagonally across, the very old man has two. "Maybe you can—"

Konrad crossed over and also invited the old man, who did not understand what was wanted from him. But the beggar with the three fingers, who had been watching closely, promised he would take care of everything. Which made Konrad believe that they all had a business relationship with one another.

So he asked the others to come over for the evening: the beggar without a nose or chin and the one whose thigh stumps were strapped to a board with wheels.

He was now intent on leaving the blaring site of all this merrymaking, but then he saw the hunchback who had earlier been thrown out of Phantomata's domain leaning against one of the trees that stood by the end tents.

Konrad went up to him. Somehow he belongs with the festivities of the coming hours, he thought; I want to ask him; he can continue to devote himself to this

Fräulein Phantomata. And, taking off his hat, Konrad asked whether he had injured himself in the fall.

The deformed man shook his undamaged hump and pointed over to the open stand of a throwing game. He was already feeling indignant again: there, too, they were cheating and vulgarizing. "Never—oh never does the circlet fall over the coveted bottle in such a way that the saucer is enclosed by the hoop. Every mark gambled is lost. Because—a very simple swindle—the rings are sized to the same width as the saucers, so they always get stuck and never fall over them."

He pulled Konrad closer and ran his thin hand into the breast pocket of his baggy overcoat. There he had his own rings that he had made just yesterday. They were of the prescribed size and offered the skilled player every honorable opportunity to win. "Oh, they are only half a centimeter larger than the swindling rings of the crook over there! When you get the useless ones handed to you, you have to swap them quickly, and tomorrow and every day after that again and again swap newly made ones for the fraudulent ones, until the entire bogus inventory of the old crook has been changed into an honest business without him knowing. Would you like to try it?" As for him, he had practiced at home and was certain that he would win a bottle of wine with every throw.

They went over. Konrad covered the exchange. The hunchback did as he had predicted. Konrad was amazed at the dogged self-assurance with which he replaced the cheating rings with the fair ones and so snatched one bottle of wine and schnapps after the other from the astonished ring game owner.

The hunchback told Konrad that he would only take all of these with him if he had guests, and he loaded Konrad with all the bottles. He did not win them for himself, he said; they are intended as an involuntary toll, paid by the crook to the general public.

Konrad asked him to come to his gathering, and the other promised to do so with a fond farewell, in which he stated very formally that he would therefore have to change his clothes.

Konrad went back into town. A wind that had blown down from the stars and strayed into the streets of men ushered him home, while a solitary paper rustled and ran alongside him in the strong breeze—a silent companion who did him ghostly benefaction.

He realized that this evening would have to take on the character of a painful orgy. Once home, he boiled water over the fire for grog and mulled wine.

The first to tug the bell was the blind man. "The gentleman needn't be surprised," he said. The last surgical procedure had given him back part of his sight for a short time. It wasn't worth changing the painted iron signboard that read "poor blind man"; that endless night would soon return.

Konrad sat him down in a corner of the sofa where he was satisfied with bread and cheese. He had never lived beyond his means, he said, and his final years were taken care of. His son Karl will bring his barrel organ along with his own.

Konrad learned that his son Karl was the one who, all totaled, had three remaining fingers.

Karl arrived with the barrel organs hanging from him, and next to him was the legless man on the wheel board, who pushed himself forward with his hands. Son Karl knocked on the window and unceremoniously heaved the heavy burden of the strapped-on cripple through the open window into Konrad's arms.

"It's good that the gentleman doesn't live three flights up," Karl announced. "We have three discs of 'Liebeslust.'" Using his chin and nose and the stumps of his fingers he set up the machines.

The last two beggars, who arrived with their rain-soaked clothes steaming, also brought "Liebeslust" with them.

They were already drinking warmed wine against the encroaching coolness of the autumn night when Phantomata slipped into the room.

Konrad was startled. She wore the same gray-brown-black dress a hundred thousand others wore. Brittle spots and threadbare parts were barely covered. Like the crumbling skin at her temple that, stripped of make-up, was worn to a frightening nakedness. All the same, Konrad saw the shimmering braid of the glorious blonde hair—along its edges the remnants of the ineradicable makeup. She will spread it around overnight and will have smoothed over her entire face and neck again by to-morrow, he thought. She was holding her hat in her hand as if it was too tight for her flood of hair, and he asked her if she would like him to take it. She then slipped into the free corner of the sofa and got something to drink. She kept very quiet—and smiled a dubious smile when Konrad assured her that these six gentlemen had ap-peared to make music in her honor.

But the night was not to blossom so quickly into the grand painful concert. The hunchback appeared in a respectable evening suit and meticulously starched shirt, which curved over his prominent breastbone like a white barrel. He shook hands with everyone except Kon-rad. He bowed to Konrad and announced that his name was Grodeck, then jumped up and settled in on the pil-lows with Phantomata.

Konrad announced that he also considered the evening valuable because Herr Grodeck could now continue to address the subject that he had raised so spiritedly a few hours before in Phantomata's booth, and because they could now calmly consider what needed to be done to remedy the dangers to which Phantomata's health may be exposed.

Phantomata smiled and drove her pointed tongue, which shot red as if bleeding out of her pale face, into her glass and sipped the alcohol, which the hunchback with his scolding mouth declared to be vile. He was indignant again. "Here we have a further outrage from the crook with his too tight hoops," he complained. "The fact is that he pays out with the most deplorable booze that can be imagined." He smelled the schnapps bottle. "Alcohol," he said, "but so bad that it wouldn't even catch fire in Fräulein Phantomata's curling machine."

He looked at her humbly from below, eager to see the effect of his caustic joke.

But Phantomata's eyes were focused on the shiny black mustache of the legless young soldier who was strapped to the wheel board and who squatted half under the table as if on the floor. And then she jumped up and asked whether the gentleman, who was sitting so low and completely in the dark, wouldn't like to move up a bit, and sit in the corner of the sofa for a while.

Working together, the group unbuckled the thigh stumps, and the flattered groaning man was rolled over to where Phantomata wanted him.

Only Herr Grodeck didn't participate. He got up and sat down on a chair to the side. This was a quiet declaration of war. And the beggar with the leg stumps loudly asked whether he was not refined enough for the gentleman, as the gentleman was running away from him. Over pursed lips, Phantomata shot a look full of hate and sadness into the hunchback's feebly defensive face.

The others were against him too. "The wine is good," the blind man grumbled. They drank it and the schnapps in streams. Rather, they didn't drink it—they poured it down the way you fill lamps that have burned empty and must flare up again.

Konrad saw his evening was ending before it even began. And so he insisted that at least "Liebeslust" should be heard before the beggars were unable to crank rhythmically.

While the symphony was being prepared, Konrad again raised the question of Herr Grodeck's former plan to save Phantomata from the hands of the man in the red tailcoat.

Herr Grodeck dismissed it. "Where does violence and deceit not reign? Where to start? And again, this wine is a hideous record of human meanness. Not to speak of the schnapps. Which, even if the gentlemen here like to drink it, only shows how easy wickedness in general has it."

Konrad asked Phantomata whether she really would be worn out and ready for the sanatorium in five years.

She shrugged her narrow shoulders childishly and smiled a flat, gray smile. Her hand played over the back of the sofa near the man with the black mustache. Konrad angrily told her that she shouldn't have removed her makeup. He has chalk, red chalk and oil; he wanted to get it for her so she could use it to make some make-up; she should mix everything and cover herself and her skinlessness with it.

She stood up without a word and went to the window. She seemed close to crying. Herr Grodeck joined her. Without her noticing it, he flicked a piece of bread into the thick waves of her hair. And then he asked if he could be of help to her. He had had the power to stand up to the impresario. If she wanted to leave that job, he could stand up for her alone, without the help of these other men. Also, something has gotten into her hair; if he may be allowed to pull out the foreign body out, she should stoop a little.

She did—and he dipped nervous fingers into the silky splendor. With a wicked tone of voice, he explained that it wasn't all that easy ... And he burrowed his way, trembling, deeper into a sea of supple blonde.

But the man with the leg stumps intervened. From where he is he can see where the ball of bread, which the gentleman himself had just shot into the lady's hair, was stuck. "Can't you see it?" he says. "Do you want to entirely ruin her hairdo?"

Phantomata shook Herr Grodeck out of her hair like a nasty spider. She ran over close to the mustached man and leaned in further and stayed longer in his hands than it would have taken to untangle all her curls. He had to give her a friendly poke on her forehead to get her to straighten up again, a little dizzy.

Herr Grodeck silently shoved his arms into his overcoat and buttoned it. And this silence cried out like heat and condemnation. With an innkeeper's smile, Konrad asked him to stay longer and, if the wine didn't taste good either, at least listen to "Liebeslust."

But the barrel organs, under the direction of the beggar with the three fingers, did not get off to a uniform start. They started up at a signal flourish from Konrad, but they were already shrilly confused by the fifth bar. Two shot ahead of the others and assertively stayed in the lead. The blind man's machine at first pumped only wind, then abruptly burst into an uncontrolled caterwauling.

Konrad canceled the concert. He apologized to the hunchback; he now no longer knew why he had arranged this evening.

Herr Grodeck appeared to take this badly as well, for before he left he conveyed to everyone in an exalted tone that they owed the wine, middling as it may be, the only abiding gift of the night, to him. In addition, it came to them as a result of the successful rebuke of a man who had previously only lived to shamelessly exploit his fellow men.

When the hunchback was outside, the beggar without a nose spoke for the first time. He repeated with a grunt, "The only gift of the night? But tonight there is a gift still to be given, and that is the lady; she should decide who she wants to sleep with."

"Draw lots, draw lots, draw lots!" cried the old blind man who, if she was given free choice, had no hope for himself—and alcohol drool ran down from the corner of his mouth.

Konrad was horrorstruck. Through the tobacco haze, above a gray face, he saw a shimmering tower of golden hair that breathed and outweighed every miserable torment. Should she be thrown to a pack of wild animals?

But Phantomata made a quick decision. Scurrying, she hid in the armpit of the cripple with the black beard; he was completely inundated by the blonde as she gave herself to him.

"Children, children!" the beggar with three fingers bellowed good-naturedly. "You don't want to stand in the way of the happiness of these children. They should be happy, immediately and without delay. Where is the doctor's bedroom?"

Konrad believed he owed this last thing to his unique guests, and he threw open the bedroom door.

Then the strangest thing happened. Phantomata, slender and gray, drew tremendous strength from within herself and carried the heavy lump of meat that was clutching her around the neck off to the bed.

The door of the room slammed behind her amidst the unbridled laughter of the wedding party, who, very hoarse and dry with joy, pumped the last dregs out of the bottles into themselves. They indulged themselves in vivid discussions of details. The beggar without a nose bawled against the door, asking if the delicate woman should be told to wrap up her babe in arms. The blind beggar even tried the handle, reassuring those inside that it was he, the blind man, that he didn't need to see, that he could hear everything, but he didn't hear in which hotel the couple was planning to stay tomorrow.

Then they finished off everything drinkable and said goodbye and farewell. Konrad escorted them to the house door. The night fell on him with a clatter of stars; he braced himself against the immeasurable sheen of the transcendent dark blue that stretched out endlessly. For a moment he forgot Phantomata, the rutting, and the barrel organs. Then he looked again at the beggars, sticking to the hollow-sounding pavement, staggering as they moved along at regular, constant intervals.

When he crept back into the dungeon-like room, Phantomata was standing there.

He helped lift a fallen wave of hair from her forehead. Will she marry the man in there now?

She doesn't know, wonders why he is asking. She is constantly being asked things. Why is she always being asked things! Instead of asking questions he should help her get Oskar back on the board. She wanted to go away with him. He is asleep. All that wine . . .

Together they lifted the cripple onto the wheeled cart. He woke up temporarily, babbled something, and fell asleep again in a crouch.

They pushed him out of the room, wheels creaking down the corridor and rumbling down over the stone steps.

They left him sitting in the street and went back in once more. There was no rope, so Konrad had to cut her a length of curtain cord.

Phantomata made a kind of harness out of it and hitched herself up.

Konrad watched her dragging her lover down the street.

The small wheels jangled in the early morning; cold and strange, it stretched out over them.

THE OFFERING*

An old woman crouched in devotion in the church, which was empty at the hot midday hour and thoroughly chilled by the twilight reveries of its saints.

Once she had mumbled away the last bead of the rosary, she rose with difficulty. With her bent back and sloping narrow shoulders, she was hardly taller than before and resembled a kneeling woman, still.

She thought she had prayed enough, so now thought that she would steal a little, because while God was good, life was hard. This life had been given her by people with a shrug of their shoulders, not caring about her and leaving her to starve. So she had to take care of herself as best she could. Perhaps by way of a plan that had emerged while she was fingering the rosary. Who had given it to her? she asked herself. Possibly that saint over there.

---

* The title of this story in the original, *Opfer*, has numerous meanings—"offering," "victim," and "sacrifice" among them [trans.].

It would be a mad and dangerous task to steal something from the offering box in the usual manner. But, she wondered, is it perhaps not as daring an undertaking to walk through the church, run a liming rod through the slot, and fish for copper and nickel coins?

Her work will be easier today, owing to the saint's suggestion, and at the same time it will be more profitable. She thought about how people know that they are evil and walk wicked paths; about how people have so much money—far, far more than before the war, after which they cry that it has made them poor. And about how, because people know they are bad, they like to sacrifice to the church to buy a little salvation for themselves. They sacrifice money, paper money. That's it: paper money!

She tells herself, "In the past you had to be happy with a few pennies which would stick to the rod and could then be pulled up from the bottom of the offering box into the daylight and into your pocket. Today you can fill the offering box with bulky newspaper up to the slot. What is thrown in through it remains on top, remains to a certain extent on top, so that one can easily pull it out with the thin fingers of barren existence. But . . . the coins landing on paper will not rattle, as they usually do, when they fall down on the others. Pah, people have forgotten the clatter of coins; they won't be puzzled. Paper money doesn't clatter. These days money no longer makes a hard ringing noise; these days it creeps through the world on cowardly and fibrous soles."

The old woman's head juts out from her body. She turns it side to side. Her weakening eyes search. Apart from the saints, she sees no figure in her vicinity. She does not shy away from the saints; they see into the heart of a poor woman, and into her empty stomach. They understand that someone who is not a saint has to take care of themselves a little.

The old woman carefully pulls a newspaper out of her pocket and begins to tear it up and make a ball. The wrinkled paper crackles and rustles. It frightens her and she pauses. How it echoes in the church! Could someone who has already figured it out have laughed mockingly at her beginning? She looks around again: no one is there, and the saints here don't laugh.

And yet, someone is quietly laughing. The old woman has not seen him—and does not hear him. He stands apart, in the shelter of pious darkness. A man. He has good eyesight and he sees the woman stuffing bulky paper into the offering box.

Her hands rush; she barely manages it. And she is not sure whether she did it well, whether the ball of paper is placed correctly. The coins will be able to slide into the depths left and right of it. They are lost. At least then they rattle—as if everything was absolutely in order. But the banknotes! They stay there.

Tonight, when the busy visiting hours are over, she will check back and see how much she has captured.

She turns to shuffle away. Her passage through the nave becomes faster the farther she gets from the offering box. She crosses herself and stumbles out onto the white square, which blazes into her face with all its sunshine. She quickly puts on her blue glasses.

The man in the church crosses over to the place where the old woman had behaved so mysteriously. He peeks in the slot: Oh, what a clumsy swindle! He grasps it immediately.

He pulls the scrap of newspaper up a little to be absolutely sure he is not mistaken. It is difficult for his big fingers to draw the paper through the slit, but he manages. Now he could easily remove this stupid thief's invention from the offering box, and the thief, when she comes back to harvest the fruits of her labor, would be left feeling a shocked disappointment and half-certain that she had been caught. She wouldn't try pilfering ever again.

Should he do it? No. He smiles again and carefully stuffs the newspaper back into the box with all the delicacy of effort that his fat fingers are capable of. He tries very hard to restore the simple money trap exactly as it had been. Perhaps he'll be able to sort the paper even more effectively than the old woman with shaky fingers? He does so.

Then he leaves, without praying, without crossing himself. He's still smiling. But even though he only smiles very thinly, doesn't his face look as if it is wholly distorted by greed?

Greed drives the old woman back to her church before it's late enough in the evening that the prime visiting hours are over. She has to observe, to see whether the offering box is doing a good business.

The church is full of seekers of God, joyfully leaving, because supper beckons them—a table of meat and beer. The old woman also hopes for a better evening; that will depend on the outcome of her invention; perhaps today she can buy a piece of that cheese that is soft and easy to chew.

She stands and listens; she doesn't watch with her eyes because she doesn't see well enough. Now bending at the prayer bench, she hears the departing people going past her, toward and then past her offering box. She hears the ticking falling of coins. Coins only? Let them tick away! What falls in silently and stays on top is better. She giggles a bit. Her jaws chomp, as if they are already enjoying that cheese. Patience!

The man is back, too. He stands very close to the offering box. He is no less eager to watch than she is. He's smiling again. Only coins fall in, slide away from the paper and clink against the bottom. Ah, the old woman's gimmick doesn't seem to be of any use. Will her dirty trick be exposed in the end? In the end he decides he has to help it along.

He has an idea that makes him grin proudly. He pulls out his wallet, chooses the cleanest mark notes from it, three bills, then wets a pencil with eager lips, and with the bills braced against the church wall, carefully writes a word or two on each of the notes. He lets the notes disappear into the outer pocket of his coat, where they are ready for quick access, and he waits.

He closely watches the hands of the donating women. No bill is delivered into the slot. He sees only coins slide in; he sees this clearly and hears a regular ticking. How ridiculous the old thief's mistaken calculation is! Content, he deciphers the inscription on the offering box: "For the Neglected Youth" is written there in artless white letters. So, she wanted to deprive the neglected youth of their money! You have to admit, this is quite a trick!

The old woman grows restless. Her eagerness for the loot keeps her from staying on the prayer bench. It drives her up and away from the site of her deed. She thinks she will look suspicious if she remains in the same place, listening.

The man feels something close to shock as he watches her walk away. She won't want to give up her little swindle, will she? Has he anticipated something in vain; stood waiting in vain?

But the old woman doesn't leave the church. She limps over to the other side. More people seem to be streaming along this parallel aisle—past another offering box and out. Perhaps she would have done better to choose this side for her purposes; it is evidently the richer side. But she knows that it is meant for the poor of the city, and she has wanted to avoid reducing its take. In the end she would get a little out of this fund herself. Now, however, when she thought she saw that benevolence flowed more freely here than for the neglected youth over there, she almost regretted her choice.

Her minder never lets her out of his sight. And he immediately gets why she is lurking near the offering box. She has fitted this one with her invention as well! Not just one, which would be just petty thievery, which no one would condemn too harshly, but all the boxes of the church, with the boldest impudence. Big business! Who could deny that one has a sacred duty to take action against such a character!

Gradually the church regains the deep twilight appearance of its echoing seclusion. The last people walk under the portal that leads out into blue evening.

Now it is important for the man to be very careful so that he doesn't miss the right moment.

Here she comes, the thief, hesitantly approaching. He is surprised that she didn't feel around in the offering box over there. Does she want to check this one for the haul first? Is he standing in her way? I'll leave in a moment, dearest. Just one moment more!

He pulls the bills out of his coat pocket, lets them slide into the box, with the gentle and pious movement of one making an offering, crosses himself at the holy water font and walks on, head bowed. The old woman can rest assured that everything is fine.

He walks around a thick pillar that conceals him, pulls open a door and waits until it thuds back against the leather padding, turns and tiptoes into the gloomy depths to the side and stands exactly where he stood at noon that day watching the old woman.

Oh, she's already fingering into the offering box, throwing her angular head with weak eyes to the left and right, like a bird trying to strike out with its beak.

The man is ready to spring. Only, by God, he doesn't want to grab her too soon! The old carcass has to have the spoils firmly in her claws; otherwise she will deny everything later. He sees that she is wrapping something in a dirty little cloth; she puts it in her pocket.

Staggering, she turns to go; she has succeeded in her task. She feels free, unburdened. To be freed this way makes her for the moment happier than the money gained by way of her cunning does. She is staggering still because this first theft scared the hell out of her.

Then the man springs to her in three leaps. She sees the devil springing through the church toward her. He doesn't even need to take her in hand—she falls over by herself.

He has to help her stand up. "Admit everything," he says.

She begs and whimpers. She gestures with her hands: she wants to go out there—into the balmy evening—away from him, not into prison. "Oh, dear sir, not into prison."

"Just come with me," the man says coldly, all business. "Just calm down," he says in a condescending tone that he believes will make her more docile. "This won't cost you your head. Come on, come on, come on," he drones.

She lets him push her. Words keep falling from her mouth, a confused babble. He doesn't listen.

"I'll hand you over to the first policeman," he says. "Then, for me, this thing will be done. We will have nothing else to do with one other. I'll be on my way."

He finds one immediately, standing where he should be, on the square in a peaceful evening. When the old woman sees the formidable upright symbol of retaliation, she tries to run away. It is a completely ridiculous attempt.

"I have a thief here to pass along to you," the gentleman explains to the policeman, who salutes benevolently, and is ready to officially take charge.

The gentleman tells the policeman the story of the offering box in detail. The policeman smiles appreciatively at the revelations of cunning and counter-cunning. Good has triumphed; the stranger deserves respect.

He adds for emphasis: "No ordinary thief, you understand, but a very cunning one. Can you believe it? She arranged all the offering boxes, five in number, in her shameful way for her robbery."

The old woman, who has meanwhile managed to follow the conversation between the two men a little, shakes her head so desperately, as if she wants to shake it off her thin neck. "One, one, only one!" she wails.

"And now show us what you have stolen," says the man in a grand manner, and the policeman immediately guesses that something very special is coming now.

"I only gave her time to ransack one offering box, but I set it up so that it was the right one," says he who captured the criminal. And to her, who falls silent again and trembles in the evening completely uncomprehending, "You wrapped the stolen money in a handkerchief, put the handkerchief in your apron. I know everything. Hand it over."

The old woman obediently unfolds her handkerchief. Four mark notes appear in the evening light. The man snatches them from her.

"You see, here," he says with a wide face and taking a wide stance, reveling in his clever victory. "What does it say here, on three of these notes? 'Josef Richtlinger' is clearly written here. Three times. Once on each note. My name, my money. Surely this is—so to speak—certain conviction of the thief, eh?"

"Yes," the policeman admits respectfully.

"This was especially important in the event that she should deny the theft," the man explained about his system of entrapment. "But she doesn't deny it at all." He seemed sorry about that.

"One mark," the old woman said, "one mark is mine. One mark . . ."

The man laughed heartily. "The fourth mark, eh? No, my smart one, we won't fall for it. Look how clever you are! My name is not on it, but that mark comes from the offering box."

"I had it!" blubbers the old woman. "I had it before. It's mine! Oh, all my money!"

The two men laugh together. They understand one another.

The cunning man claps his big hands. "So that's it!" he announces. And he decides to make a joke: he tells the policeman, "Get home safely with your lady." But before they split up, something else occurs to him: "I would like to take my three marks with me now. It has clearly been proven that they belong to me! You have my details, should the court need me."

The policeman hastens to highlight the importance of his testimony: "The court certainly will need you later at the hearing." And then, blinded by the man's achievements, he hands over the three one-mark notes.

They part. The policeman almost has to carry the old woman. She stumbles over the dark swells of her fear. How desolately the disheveled gray skirt hangs loosely around her hips! The little white braid has come loose from her skull and waves in the night for help.

But next to her the uniformed man is triumphant, blue and erect. Something flashes about her; it is the sparkling pure sword of righteousness.

THE EXCHANGE

———

Late, as always, Edith arrived at the opera.

The eyebrow pencil had rolled under the vanity table and hidden there. The choice between the silk and the patent leather shoes had been difficult and time-consuming. Should she choose the ruby or the emerald for the beautiful declivity between her breasts?

But now this was all happily behind her and she has arrived.

For a moment she hesitated; the veil of snowflakes that fell in front of the little window of the car held her back. If she hadn't decided to forgo the fur-lined overshoes she had at home, it would have been easier now to take the few snowy steps to the shelter of the entrance.

Then a hand reached through the veil of snow and opened the car door. So she felt compelled to get out, for better or for worse. She stepped past the shapeless, hooded, white-covered creature before her, and handed the driver, who had remained in his seat, a banknote, far in excess of adequate payment. She immediately turned away, to avoid being here in the cold, which was already nipping at the soles of her shoes, a second longer than necessary.

But the hooded figure that she had wanted to leave behind was plucking at her evening cloak, and a voice, simultaneously demanding and humble, called out something like: "Please, my lady . . ."

Edith, sheltered now in the entrance, turned around unwillingly. So many delays!

A young woman opened a gray shawl and revealed an infant deep in the crook of her supporting arm. The free hand stretched out, demanding; Edith looked into this empty, shallow, slightly trembling bowl. Not even gloves, she thought. Pity rose uncomfortably.

She quickly said, "Certainly, Fräulein—or no: you are probably married—that's right, you were the one who opened the car door; take—"

She fished for coins in the bottom of her beaded bag. When she tried to load the frosty begging hand with it, it all fell. Both women had to bend down, the headscarf of the poor woman slipped away, their heads touched; blonde hair, tightly and carelessly knotted, and blonde hair, carefully waved, but sparser beneath a diadem, flowed into one another.

The infant tipped forward in the supporting arm, woke up and cried out loudly.

Edith straightened up. She saw that the beggar woman possessed a disheveled beauty, buried, as it were, under the rubble of poverty, and a body that was about the same size as her own. The same arching of the brow that bedevils a man like a threatening archway to happiness—only here without the aid of a pencil. She saw hair that was richer and more shimmering and golden than her own, and an ear surely no less beautiful because not a drop of stone sparkled in it.

"Why are you begging," she asked harshly. "Isn't the child freezing? Quiet it down. Don't you have a husband who works and earns money?"

The other shrugged her gray shoulders.

For a moment Edith imagined the woman opposite—her antagonist—clad in the splendor of her own silk, saw her hips wrapped in it, shining, saw her in sparkling jewels, fragrant, redolent of satiety. An image that challenged. An image that—realized—might not even have been ridiculous.

"Are you freezing that badly, or are you shaking—for other reasons?" Pretending, she thought—a trick of her trade.

Another shrug. Then she defiantly murmured: "It's cold. I've been standing here for an hour."

"Why has it been that long? Theatergoers don't come that early, do they?" At least not distinguished visitors, she told herself. She ran her hand over the hair of the child, whose crying had grown quieter and more desperate. The mother flinched and pulled a corner of the shawl over the little head.

"I'm not allowed to touch it?" Edith laughed scornfully, out of embarrassment. "Do you think I mean to poison it?" She felt greed for the child of the lowly woman, which had been taken from her so abruptly.

"I'm not just standing here because of the theater people," conceded the beggar. "Passersby also come down the street. Some give something."

"Some give something," repeated Edith, sensing how pitiful these monetary gains must be. "How much—I mean, on average?"

A shrug—and silence. The curiosity of the rich! I see through them! So said the look of the silent, hostile one.

Edith lowered her eyes. Why can't I leave? she thought. What do I want from this one? "There's still money here from my—from what I—" And with the delicate tip of her shoe she touched a fallen coin.

The beggar did not bend down. Edith had to pick up the money herself, and the other meanwhile said scornfully: "You are missing your play. And you're freezing; you aren't used to being outdoors."

I am freezing, thought Edith, and felt an ambiguity about the word. It must in some manner make you feel happy and warm to hide a little screamer like that under a scarf, against your chest.

"—although the cloak you're wearing," said the darkly rebellious voice of the poor woman, "may keep you warm. Heavy silk, is it?"

"This cloak?" Edith said dismissively. "Oh, there are others that are better protection." There are three that are warmer, she was ashamed to say. I don't lack much; what am I lacking? Rudolf sits in the box and waits. Maybe he hasn't been waiting inside for all that long. If I go in now, he'll grin and whisper: "Late, as always! A big dress rehearsal at home—for the performance within the performance, of course." I know those nasty words by heart. He only sees my delay; he doesn't see me. What am I missing out on if I stay here with this beggar? It's the same music every time. He makes the same music every time. Disgusting. Am I freezing? It's actually quite good to be cold—if you are already cold inside. What is it like to beg—when you are already begging inside?

"Still not leaving?" pressed the young woman. Her child began to snivel again. She took a pacifier out of her skirt pocket and stoppered its sobbing mouth. "Damn brat," she hissed through pursed lips.

Edith was shocked. "I thought you loved it. I wasn't allowed to touch it earlier, and now you're cursing it?"

Shrug. "I don't know," she said helplessly, looking down and out into the darkness of the street. Then, tormented by the rich woman's intrusive and puzzling refusal to move away: "Don't you want to go inside, where it's warm and bright? I've heard that you can even get something to eat inside."

Edith once more embraced the figure of the beggar—and a decision was made. "No, I'll stay here," she said hastily and firmly, "and you'll go in."

The beggar beamed, closed her eyes in disbelief at the sparkling she already saw herself surrounded by. Then she straightened up as if she were already walking through the ranks of antagonists, with whom she now belonged.

"Here, take my cloak!" Edith hastened to add. "Do you think that I can't stand there like you, with the child in my arms for a few hours, and reach out my hand to the passersby? You just have to lend me your shawl. Oh, look, it's not all that thin, and it covers you from top to bottom. And you can also take my lace scarf and wrap your hair with it. You should pull a strand a little way down on your forehead. You have really wonderful hair; Rudolf will be amazed if he asks—no, before he can even ask, tell him only 'Edith sent me!' Take my bag as well. In it you'll find my pass for the first balcony, fourth box, and you must of course eat the chocolate!"

The beggar surrendered her will under the lady's directing hands. She was already transformed.

"You are beautiful," said Edith softly, beginning to doubt the wisdom of what she was doing. "You may even be more beautiful than me." But the dreamy smile of the poor woman revealed bad teeth. That outweighs everything; this makes everything right again. Edith felt happy and reassured.

"Give me the child! You must not take the child into the box with you!" She laughed then.

The beggar, in a waking dream, also allowed this to be lifted from her arms. She was already staggering in, as if in a daze, and Edith called after her: "We'll meet again out here."

Alone now, she began to settle in. Tuck the scarf lower over your forehead so it's sure to cover that silly hair accessory! Which hand should she stretch out? The right arm cradled the child. So the left. She slipped the rings from her left fingers onto her right.

The baby under the cloth warms her: I thought as much. Somehow a child warms that way. It's not so very cold; it would be even more comfortable if you crouched down.

She brushed the snow off the steps to the entrance, crouched, turning the infant in the hollow of her lap, gathering the cloth over her knees, and keeping her bare hand ready to thrust out for a donation.

But she had to learn that there were constables who conscientiously enforced the rules of the wealthy. Don't sit around here, they say. Move along! they say.

She stood and walked a few steps to the wall of the adjoining house, leaning against it; her armpit touched the protruding drainpipe. A tiny corner, a hint of a corner, but better than being at the mercy of the open area.

Never in my life have I stood in the shelter of a drainpipe. The world looks very different from here.

Good. If only my child doesn't start crying. Here comes a man; not a policeman. A donor, perhaps.

But she stretched out the narrow back of her hand as if it were a gracious gesture or to invite a kiss on the hand, forgetting to form the begging bowl—and the passerby hesitated, marveled for an uncertain moment at the white lily, strangely blossoming out of the slit of a gray shawl, and then walked on.

"I'm poor," Edith said derisively after him. "No one gives me anything. Am I really poor? With all the glitter and jewelry about my body? It gives me the lie. I need to make myself poorer."

She felt the soft stirring of the child's limbs, little legs that pressed against her breast in its sleep.

"The new beggar mama wants to make a good haul for the little prince," she said tenderly, looking down and into the opening in the cloth, from which a musty smell rose, as if from an animal's den.

She tore the tiara from her head with a single pull, and some hair went with it; she tore at the beads around her neck; she put all her rings in a palm of her hand; but while taking off her bracelets she had to lean the infant against her feet for a moment.

She had all her jewelry gathered up now. She slipped it behind the child's laced swaddling clothes. A fairy gift, she thought. My boy, we are both poor, but one of us was visited in the dark of night by the well-known, kind fairy, disguised as a miserable mother, and given glittering presents.

Then the child began to cry. The pacifier had fallen. She had to pick it up out of the trampled snow.

She was frightened. She didn't know how to fit a pacifier into a small open mouth, which was emitting clouds of vapor into the icy air, without it falling into its depths and, swallowed, would certainly be deadly. She remained helpless.

Someone was coming again. Two men, talking. It's a good thing he's screaming too, she hopes. "A donation, sir!"

The conversation tramps past her: "—all the same, after such reflection there would still be a willingness—" She remains unnoticed, meaningless words from these men fall into her ear. Pass through.

The child was crying its head off, writhing like a chopped-off segment of a worm—and she understood the cause of the severe discomfort to be the gold and gems under the swaddling, which she had let slide down and which were now probably pressing into tender flesh.

"Wealth is hard—do you feel it?" She smiled. "This, my boy, is even more important: wealth makes you hard." She carefully pushed all the hardness that she could get hold of from the outside through the covering down past tiny ribs and curves, shook the bundle—and let all of it slip down into the sack formed by the material below the child's feet.

The child grew quiet. She managed to put the pacifier into the exhausted mouth. He began sucking, a soft smacking she listened to enviously.

"Suck it some for me."

People on the street again. Husband and wife, furtive, in a hurry. "A contribution, sir?" Now the hand forms the bowl. But to no avail.

Is she doing it wrong? Should she have said, "Please, madam!" Women are more compassionate. Are they? Is that why she is standing here? Out of pity? Out of pity for herself.

The beggar woman was sitting above her, in the warm glow of a large house. Right next to Rudolf, who had to put up with this one from the alley being right next to him, who bore this like a cross that had to be dragged through a three-act opera. Who suffered more, she below in the snow—or he above? Whose life was more painful?

"My boy," she said tenderly, hugging the baby. How long it had been since she had last whispered "my boy" to him up there! Wasn't it a generation ago? Compared to that endlessly distant time, what did all the endlessness of this hour on the snow-blown street mean? Hadn't she been lost to him—become a stranger at a cool distance—long ago? So, truly, a generation has passed.

It's very cold! My toes are numb flesh. Chilblains will clothe me strangely. But I don't even know what that looks like. There is so much I don't know; one does learn. Is the child freezing? I'll be prosecuted for infanticide.

People passing closely from both directions. Their warmed voices ringing in the beggar's icy ear, the beggar's freezing voice soundless in deaf ears: "Please, sir!—Oh, madam, we beg you!—Fräulein!" . . . Past.

The child is not cold at all. Edith's fingers feel contented stirrings in its sleep. If I were in your place! The world would bloom celestially for me! Rudolf is sitting upstairs, next to the lower-class woman. He can't get over his deep uneasiness. How humiliated he feels! Did she let the lace shawl slip down? She keeps her cloak tightly closed to hide her rags. A little ridiculous, isn't it? Oh, how embarrassing, to sit in the box with such a lady! But during the intermission the three thousand hearts of the thoroughly inflamed chamber stir at the abundance of vigorous blonde hair the likes of which only she possesses. Rudolf sees it. Her gaze is more animal than mine; men love that. Rudolf has to smile excitedly, to the detriment of his genteel anger—driven by the urge of all males within him. But she smiles too, humbly audacious, and that's good. He sees her neglected teeth. That's good.

I'm doing this wrong. I have to tell those who pass by: "The child is ill; two more at home are starving; the fourth is already growing in my belly. And the man who is to blame for all this limps through the room with only one leg, cleans tables with only one arm—which benefits me; he can only hit me with half his strength. But his meager war invalid's pension cries out to heaven. Oh, sir, a ten-mark bill, otherwise I'll throw myself into the water!"

Otherwise I'll throw myself into the water; it wouldn't be entirely unreasonable. Will this night on the street, this night of begging, never end? Haven't the fine rogues up there heard enough opera? How long do we have to wait until Rudolf comes out? I want to eat something, chicken with asparagus tips. How tenderly he will put my cloak around my shoulders, here next to the rain gutter! That beggar woman's rag won't infest me with vermin! Afterward, we'll laugh a little, Rudolf and I, because of the masquerade we've gone through. But our laughter has become so strange—

Edith notices that the snow is no longer dusting the street. The expanse is glistening with purified air. Lanterns stab crossly at the beggar woman. Snow crystals reflect a thousand-fold. She is tired, ready and willing to lie down in it. All the lights of the big house are reflected in the hair of those up there . . . And what about Rudolf's willingness? . . . Would there still be a willingness after such reflection? . . . She remembers the snippet of conversation from the mouth of someone who hurried by. Meaningless words—as she believed earlier? Oh no: a most meaningful word!

But—actually—the theater is emptying out now! Shameful for you to have to lie to your counterpart: I didn't earn anything. After all, the fairy's gift will be found in the brat's dirty diapers.

Perhaps I'll get something at the last minute! And she holds out the hollow of her narrow hand to the streamers, completely in shadow and completely masked—acquaintances can walk by. But these animals scurry away heedlessly, hungering for conveyances, for chicken with asparagus tips, for bed and embrace.

There is Rudolf! Finally! Hasn't he torn the cloak off the woman's shoulders yet? Doesn't he have it ready for her, her cloak?

Actually, the whore struts beside him as if she belongs. How she struts! Now it's time to step into the light, now it's time! She can't. No, now it is a question of being sought and found. And she stands there.

I won't call out to him. Maybe he doesn't know I'm waiting. She didn't tell him anything. But doesn't the mother want her child back?

She extends it out from under the shawl. She sees the two smile at one another—locking eyes, nothing on the street is there for them any longer.

They step up to a car ... The way she gathers her cloak—as if I were doing it myself!

Oh, he could know where I'm standing. He will know! Because she knows.

Not a glance, not a turn, not a shrug of his shoulders in my direction. And the whore gets in.

He slips in after her, greedy and bouncing, as if he were already slipping into a bed ...

Edith watches the car rolling away, getting smaller as it does. Her eyes, the light gone from them, turn away and her gaze drops.

People are still trudging past the gray shawl. "We are poor," she says. Now she extends the begging hand. And an iron coin falls in, donated by a man in a black cloak whose silk lapels curve against it. He flashes above and below, top hat and lacquer. He's gone.

She collapses, crouches next to the gutter. She feels the child heavy and soft in her lap—and her hands want to push it away, push it out, but they stroke it.

POOR

Poor Turu stood on a dust-gnawed street and stared thirstily into the green, vast velvet of a park that swelled luxuriantly up to the fence that imperiously separated wealth from desolate misery.

Inside, Gül the rich man strolled along the finely sanded park paths. Nor did he shy away from walking in the middle of the pliant lawn, which lovingly tolerated his Moroccan leather shoes.

Turu looked on. Here someone could crush flowers with impunity, while he would never be allowed to walk around here even well behaved. With a sigh he laid his head on the wrought iron vines.

Who did these flowers belong to? God had allowed them to grow, not the rich man. Could he kill them treading with his careless feet if God had not created them? And hadn't God created them? And had God created them just for the rich man to trample on? Didn't they belong to everyone?—Resentment rose in Turu.

Rich Gül walked near the fence. He looked up, he looked out through the bars at poverty and drought.

"You're tearing up my flowers," Turu couldn't help but cry out, trembling. At Gül's angry, questioning expression, he corrected himself: "Our flowers."

Gül walked over, put his gaunt hands high on the iron bars; his yellow leather face looked silently at the poor man as if from a dungeon.

Turu said, humbly now, "Forgive me, sir, hunger confuses me and makes me bold. There's no sense in talking to you like that. You don't know the irritating feeling of gaping entrails."

"Hunger," Gül repeated, as if remembering. "Yes, yes, hunger. You're wrong, I too know it." Suddenly he came alive: "Do you want something to eat? Come in! Do you want something to drink?" He strode swiftly along the fence, and so did Turu. They walked at the same pace, their bodies close together, separated only by the bars, until Gül reached a small gate in the iron, which he opened.

Turu doffed his hat and stepped through.

"You're no less outdoors than you are out there," Gül grinned at him. "Cover yourself."

Embarrassed and delighted, Turu followed his host, whose silk robe swept ahead. Softly, as if on clouds, my weariness strides effortlessly, he thought. I'm halfway to heaven! A balm of coolness wafted over him. From the flowing stillness of shrubs covered in colors birdcalls blossomed down.

Gül clapped his hands—made waving gestures. And as if he were pulling dolls on invisible strings, servants scurried toward him. He ordered that the table immediately be set for the hungry Turu. "Enjoy. And if you'd like, come here to the park every day at this hour and eat! What is your profession?"

"Stonebreaker, presently without position. And you?" asked Turu.

"I don't eat," Gül confessed tonelessly, as if it were his shame. "I have a stomach ailment. A bowl of oatmeal every day, two forkfuls of chicken; that's it. I'm going to get a massage." And he disappeared in the direction of a house that shimmered resplendently through the green of the trees.

As soon as he was gone, a table with food appeared on the lawn, conjured up by silently scurrying servants.

Turu was glad to be left all alone; now he could dig in in full freedom. As he boned the fluffy flesh of a crispy fish that fell apart blindingly white before him, he was already devouring with his nose the sweet smell of a tart next to it, and with his eyes the juicy curves of shining fruit. He was about to put the first small heap of fish into his mouth when a noise behind his chair made him look around. Horror! Above him two gigantic monkeys broke through the branches and threw themselves down upon the table with terrible grimaces.

Turu overturned everything; he jumped up in desperation. For a moment he stood there, as if caught up in the allure of the meal, then he fled from the animals. He felt as if quiet, sickly laughter sounded behind him.

A daring glance back told him that the monkeys were picking up large pieces of the cake. He couldn't find the gate. Afterward he couldn't have said how he managed to climb over the high latticework with the glittering gold uninjured.

As if in derision, the animals extended chunks of cake through the bars, smirking and with erratic gestures. Exhausted from fear and doubly in need of refreshment, he escaped.

Along the way he dug in his pocket and found a few pennies. With them he went into the cheapest tavern in town and asked for bread, an onion, and salt.

An acquaintance who was drinking stale beer— Somel the shoemaker—sat down with him. "Why so sweaty? Have you been working hard?" he asked.

Turu narrated his adventure in the garden of the rich Gül.

Somel let the thirsty man drink freely and declared: "You just have to approach it differently. I, for example, have made a big decision to finally achieve something. Today I bought an expensive lottery ticket with all my savings. My wife dreamed the exact numbers three times in a row. I am certain to win a large sum."

"And if you don't win?" considered Turu.

"We have to win," Somel said gloomily. "God cannot allow me to squander what little I have saved. Would He give us such a hint and let it turn out to be wrong?"

Turu, doubtful, didn't want to argue. They sat silent for a while, then parted.

The next day, after spending long hours of it starving, Turu again stood before the rich Gül's bars. And again, Gül walked across the lawn. Turu, anxious and shy owing to the intensity of the memory, wanted to withdraw, but Gül came closer, and the mere approach of the rich man froze him. Gül lifted his sickly face to the bars and, smiling, said, "Well?"

"Nothing," Turu replied with effort.

"Didn't you enjoy yourself last night," Gül said, and his painfully contorted mouth seemed to twitch with amusement.

"No," Turu asserted; he was determined to say nothing about the monkeys and his escape. But because Gül's mocking eyes showed he already knew everything, he confessed.

The rich man chuckled benevolently: "Dear man, it wasn't all that bad. It wasn't bad at all. It was all as it should be. The animals in my park are tame. You yourself say the monkeys rushed after you with pieces of the cake. I understand. But they meant you no harm; they meant well; they wanted to give you what was yours. Do you want to eat today? Come in!" Again, as on the day before, he strode swiftly along the fence, Turu likewise. They hastened along at the same pace, their bodies close together, separated only by the bars, until Gül once again opened the gate to his guest.

Before calling the servants, he said earnestly: "If any animals visit you today, don't be afraid. Show them that you're the master and they will obey and not trouble you."

"Stay with me!" asked Turu uncertainly, at the risk of having to mind his table manners.

Gül shook his head—and he looked as if he would have liked to stay. "I can't," he said, "my stomach—."

Turu made a difficult decision: "Couldn't I be allowed to dine in your illustrious palace? Perhaps just a bite, and very quickly?"

"In—my—house," Gül said very slowly. "Oh, you would be much more frightened there than here in this innocuous garden, under the open sky, where things are familiar." And he turned away. Turu watched him go and saw in his sluggish gait how sickness was being carried into a house of marble and gold.

The servants flew into action. The green, shimmering park evening quickly came to frame a table laden with a juice-basted roast beef and trimmings. Turu put his chair on the opposite side, so that monkeys wouldn't fall on his back when they swooped down again. When he cut the broad loin warm blood spurted out at him— but he had to look up now because something wildly striped was creeping up along the side. A big cat sat there, a tigress by her markings. She looked on with bright green eyes, now at the roast and now at Turu.

He jumped up and bowed with exaggerated politeness—already sweating but resolute. Then it occurred to him that he needed to be clearer, so he grabbed his empty plate and threw it at the tigress's skull. Shaking off the ridiculous clattering of the shards, she growled: Stop that nonsense! Then she clawed the roast off the table. Turu's fear was outweighed by his anger at being cheated again, and so, being the master here, he put his foot on the roasted piece of meat, which was his. But with a half-playful growl she took a swipe at his leg. Full of horror, he looked at his flesh wound, its flowing red; he knew that fresh blood enraged predators—and he ran.

As he hurriedly scrambled over the high fence—no time to look for the gate—Gül stepped out of the bushes. "Where are you going so quickly and clumsily?" he asked, smiling. Turu got to safety first. Then he scolded Gül through the bars from the street: "Sir, there was a tigress that is very wild—not at all tame. You lied to me. And I didn't get anything to eat."

"She's very tame," Gül contradicted scornfully. "But I've been watching you and her. You've done everything wrong. You've been behaving like Turu the stonebreaker: first cowering, then puffed up, and finally foolishly. By the time good Sakana had the meat in her claws, you had already lost it, long before. You must learn how to have a rich meal in a park. Come back tomorrow; come every evening. The table will always be set for you."

Turu hesitated, felt tired, then he wanted to shout out his defiance. But in the end he spoke softly: "Sir, I give up. I will eat my bread on the street. Of what use is a park like this to me!"

"Of what use is a park like this to me," Gül repeated darkly, pressing his temples between the bars as if he wanted to pass through. "Then go!" he suddenly cried out in melancholy anger. "Go back to your hungry existence, ingrate."

Turu slipped away. He took one furtive look back. Gül's pale head hung behind the bars as if he were a prisoner.

In the tavern he met Somel. He had drinks in front of him. He wasn't drinking and he barely nodded.

"Hey, Somel!" Turu was elated to be able to distract himself from his own suffering. "A fortune in the offing and you are as gloomy as a dead man on the gallows!"

"Won and lost," grumbled Somel the shoemaker.

"Impossible!" Turu shouted irritably, thinking Somel was teasing.

"True," Somel lamented. "It's the woman's fault: 'I'll buy pearls, a triple string. Ten silk dresses: three red, three green, two white, two blue. Plus four lap dogs and a golden purse like very fine ladies have.' She chattered on that way for hours. 'Really? Jewels around that dirty neck—with no money left for soap to wash it? Where will you hang your fine clothes? Up on the crumbling wall of the only room? Nothing remains for improving the apartment, nothing to buy cupboards and cabinets.' 'All the winnings are mine,' she shouted. 'I can do what I want with them! Because I dreamed the number. None of that money is yours.' 'I am the man, I will decide!' I yelled at her. Quarreling and yelling like that all night and far into the day. So I tore up the ticket and I burned it. Now that I am a little rested, I will go, and I will beat her." He pushed himself away from the table and went out the door.

Silence. Then Turu got up as well. He raised his arms—and he let them fall again: "Are we damned to always remain poor?"

W. C. Bamberger has translated works by Paul Scheerbart, Oscar A. H. Schmitz, and Bess Brenck Kalischer, among others. His published essays have addressed subjects ranging from the language of poet Anne Carson to the death of Kierkegaard to Guy Davenport's "friendly trees." His ebook *The Reflective Head*, on Michael Ayrton's large 1972 sculpture, is available from *Raft Magazine*. He lives in Michigan.